JORDAN

MAJOR WORLD NATIONS
JORDAN

Susan Whitehead

Corunna Middle School
LIBRARY MEDIA CENTER
400 N. Comstock
Corunna, MI 48817

CHELSEA HOUSE PUBLISHERS
Philadelphia

Chelsea House Publishers

Copyright © 1999 by Chelsea House Publishers,
a division of Main Line Book Co.
All rights reserved.
Printed in Hong Kong

First Printing.

1 3 5 7 9 8 6 4 2

Library of Congress Cataloging-in-Publication Data

Whitehead, Susan.
Jordan / Susan Whitehead
p. cm. — (Major world nations)
Includes index.
ISBN 0-7910-4980-9
1. Jordan—Juvenile literature. I. Title.
II. Series.
DS153.W48 1998
956.95—dc21   98-7530
CIP
AC

ACKNOWLEDGEMENTS

The author and publishers are grateful to the following organizations and individuals for permission to reproduce copyright illustrations in this book:
J. Allan-Cash Photo Library; Hutchison Photo Library; The Mansell Collection Ltd.; Helene Rogers

CONTENTS

Map		6
Facts at a Glance		7
History at a Glance		9
Chapter 1	Introducing Jordan	13
Chapter 2	The Jordanian Landscape	16
Chapter 3	Amman	24
Chapter 4	The Region's History	31
Chapter 5	The History of the Modern Kingdom	39
Chapter 6	Government	42
Chapter 7	The People	46
Chapter 8	The Year	52
Chapter 9	Family Life and Daily Routines	57
Chapter 10	Village Life and Agriculture	63
Chapter 11	Traditional Crafts	71
Chapter 12	Industry, Communications and the Economy	77
Chapter 13	Education and Health	86
Chapter 14	Jordan's Wildlife	92
Chapter 15	The Future	98
Glossary		100
Index		102

FACTS AT A GLANCE

Land and People

Official Name	Hashemite Kingdom of Jordan
Location	Middle East: lies between the Mediterranean and the Arabian Peninsula; bordered by Syria to the north, by Iraq and Saudi Arabia to the east and south
Area	35,467 square miles (91,860 square kilometers)
Climate	Desert climate; cool, rainy winters and hot, dry summers
Capital	Amman
Other Cities	Az-Zarqa, Irbid, As-Salt, Ar-Rusayfah, Al-Mafraq
Population	4.95 million
Population Density	131.7 persons per square mile (50.8 persons per square kilometer)
Major Rivers	Jordan, Zarqa, Yarmouk
Major Lakes	Dead Sea
Mountains	Jebel al-Adhriyat, Jebel al-Batra

Highest Point	Mount Rum
Official Language	Arabic
Religions	Sunni Muslims, Greek Orthodox, Greek Catholic, Roman Catholic
Literacy Rate	87 percent
Average Life Expectancy	64 years for males; 70 years for females

Economy

Natural Resources	Phosphate ore, potash, petroleum
Agricultural Products	Tomatoes, grapes, olives, oranges, cucumbers, bananas, wheat, barley
Industries	Fishing, mining, manufacturing, tourism
Major Imports	Machinery, transport equipment, food and live animals, mineral fuels, chemicals, iron, steel
Major Exports	Domestic goods, chemicals, phosphate fertilizers, fruits, vegetables, machinery, transport equipment
Currency	Jordanian dinar

Government

Form of Government	Constitutional monarchy
Government Bodies	National Assembly, composed of two legislative houses (Senate and House of Deputies)
Formal Head of State	King assisted by the prime minister

HISTORY AT A GLANCE

1250 B.C.   The Children of Israel enter the Promised Land at Jericho, north of the Dead Sea, after marching northward through present-day Jordan.

1200 B.C.   Three of the traditional twelve tribes of Israel, Gad, Manasseh, and Reuben settle east of the Jordan. The various parts of modern-day Jordan are referred to in the Old Testament as Edom, Moab, Gilead, and Ammon.

933 B.C.   After Solomon's death, his kingdom splits into a northern state of Israel and a southern state of Judah. Jerusalem is the capital of Judah and the northern kingdom builds a new capital at Samaria, on the modern-day West Bank. Most of northern Jordan is part of the kingdom of Israel.

587 B.C.   Jerusalem is destroyed and many of the Israelites are taken as captives to Babylon.

400 B.C.   The Nabataeans, a desert Arab group, incorporate Jordan in their kingdom.

323 B.C.   Alexander the Great dies and the Middle Eastern part of his empire is ruled by the descendants of his general, Seleucis. The Seleucid empire

	includes the western part of Jordan. The Seleucids maintain some control of the area until 142 BC.
140 B.C.	The Hasmoneans, a dynasty of mixed Israelite-Edomite ancestry, creates an independent Judean state, which gradually comes under Roman influence.
63 B.C.	The Romans build Jerash (ruins rediscovered 1806), now a well-preserved Roman city and top tourist attraction.
106 A.D.	Under the Emperor Trajan, most of present-day Jordan becomes the province of Arabia Petraea, named after the city of Petra.
661	The Umayyad dynasty, based in Damascus, occupies the area east of the Jordan River and builds a series of fortresses to protect the Jordan valley and Jerusalem from desert raiders.
750	The Umayyads are overthrown by a new dynasty, the Abbasids, who rule from Baghdad.
1086	The Seljuk Turks invade the Middle East.
1517-1519	The Ottoman Turks take control of the Middle East. They settle Circassian (European Muslims from the Caucasus) soldiers and officials in the Jordan region to guard the overland route from Turkey to Mecca, the site of Muslim pilgrimage.
1799	As part of his advance on Syria from Egypt, Napoleon occupies El Arish (February 14-15).
1916	Sharif Hussein, leader of the Hashemite clan, proclaims the Arab revolt against the Turks in Mecca. Hussein's descendants would later rule Jordan.

1917	Arab forces led by British officer T.E. Lawrence (Lawrence of Arabia) and Hussein's son Feisal capture the port of Aqaba, a key victory in the Arab revolt against the Turks.
1920	Jordan, initially known as Transjordan, emerges as a separate territory after the break-up of the Ottoman Empire. Britain administers the territory, but local government is in the hands of Amir (later King) Abdallah.
1946	Transjordan achieves full independence, and Amir Abdallah becomes King Abdallah.
1948	Jordan joins the Arab states in invading the new state of Israel. Although Israel defeats most of the invaders, the Jordan Arab Legion, led by British officers, captures East Jerusalem and the West Bank territories. Palestinian refugees are granted Jordanian citizenship.
1949	Transjordan signs an armistice with Israel (April 3). Transjordan officially changes its name to the Hashemite Kingdom of Jordan (June 2).
1951	King Abdallah is assassinated while visiting East Jerusalem. He is briefly succeeded by Amir Talal.
1952	Hussein II becomes king (May 2).
1956	King Hussein dismisses the British officers of the Arab Legion (March) and converts the Legion into an all-Jordanian force, the Jordan Arab Army.
1967	Although there is little fighting on the Jordan front during the Six-Day War, Jordan loses a great deal of territory to Israel, including East Jerusalem and the West Bank.

1970 Fighting breaks out between Jordanian military units and armed Palestinians in a conflict known as Black September. A Syrian invasion in support of the Palestinians is repulsed. After taking heavy casualties, most organized Palestinian groups withdraw to Lebanon.

1973 The October War against Israel by Egypt and Syria does not seriously affect Jordan.

1979 Israel and Egypt sign a peace agreement at Camp David, Maryland, in the United States. Since the agreement calls for an independent (non-Jordanian) West Bank, Jordan is at first hostile to the peace process.

1988 Jordan renounces all claims on the West Bank, easing relations with both Israel and the Palestine Liberation Organization.

1991 Jordan maintains neutrality in the Persian Gulf crisis and declines to join the coalition against Iraq (a former Hashemite kingdom).

1994 Jordan signs a full peace treaty with Israel.

1

Introducing Jordan

Jordan is a young country but its origins go back to the beginning of civilization. Historically, culturally and scenically its inheritance cannot be matched. It is the country from which Moses first surveyed the Promised Land and where Christ was born and died. Babylonian, Persian, Greek, Roman and Turkish forces have in turn conquered the land. Traces of the invaders and their lost cities can still be seen on the country's mountains and woods, its deserts, valleys and coral-rimmed coastline.

Jordan lies between the Mediterranean and the Arabian Peninsula. Its Arab neighbors are Syria (to the north), and Iraq and Saudi Arabia, with which it shares long desert borders to the east and south. A little further to the northwest lies the Lebanon. Jordan also has a short 15-mile (25-kilometer) coastline on the Red Sea to the south, where the narrow Gulf of Aqaba separates it from Egypt.

When the Hashemite Kingdom of Jordan was created on May 25, 1946, its western neighbor was still known as Palestine.

A Jordanian couple by the roadside—the remains of an old Crusader fortress can be seen on the hill in the background.

However, in 1948, Palestine was partitioned and the State of Israel was proclaimed in Jerusalem. War broke out between Israel and its neighbors and thousands of Palestinians fled to Jordanian territory in fear for their lives. Israel took control of much of Palestine while the area now known as the West Bank was annexed by Jordan. A second Arab-Israeli war which was fought in 1967 ended with the Israeli occupation of the West

Bank. In 1988, King Hussein renounced all Jordanian claims to the West Bank and Jordan and Israel signed a peace agreement in 1994.

Jordan is an Arab country and its people recognize close ties with the rest of the Arab world. Arabic is the official language of the country and Islam is its state religion.

An old Jordanian man. Although Jordan has been conquered and ruled by many different empires and races, it is an Arab country and its people recognize close ties with the rest of the Arab world.

2

The Jordanian Landscape

Jordan is cut in half by the Turkish-built Hejaz railway, which separates the country into barren east and fertile west. Used for transporting goods, the railway runs from Damascus, in Syria, to Aqaba, Jordan's Red Sea port. To the east of the track, a great limestone plateau slopes gently away to the deserts of east and south Jordan, Iraq and Saudi Arabia. To the west lies the western rim of the plateau, rising to heights of up to 5,400 feet (1,650 meters). These peaks were thrown up by the same violent earth movements which, millions of years ago, formed the Jordan Valley.

The valley itself is part of the Great Rift Valley, a gigantic scar in the earth's crust which runs from Lake Tiberias (the ancient Sea of Galilee) through East Africa to Lake Nyasa in southeastern Africa. The rift is a result of volcanic eruptions and the continuing shifts in the earth's surface which make themselves felt today in the slight earth tremors which occasionally disturb the region.

A view of the Dead Sea which lies between Jordan and Israel.

The road from Amman, Jordan's capital, eastward into the valley, plunges steeply down in a breathtaking series of hairpin bends as it drops abruptly down to the shores of the Dead Sea. On the way, travellers pass an incongruous sign, perched high above the valley floor but marking sea level; their ears pop with the abrupt drop in altitude; behind them and across the rift they see the scrubby limestone folds of the steep valley sides. And far below lies a green patchwork of irrigated fields. Expanses of "glasshouses"—made not of glass but of long tunnels of plastic sheeting—interrupt the greenness.

The Jordan River itself runs the length of the valley, from Lake Tiberias in the north to the Dead Sea below. Across the valley lie the mountains of the region known as the West Bank, now accessible only (with a special pass) by means of the King

Hussein Bridge. The bridge marks one of three links between the East and West Banks since Israeli forces occupied the area in 1967.

On the way south to the Dead Sea itself lies the village of Karameh, scene of a battle when Israeli forces attacked the village but were driven back by the Jordanian army and Palestinian guerrilla fighters. A war memorial marks the event.

North of this point the land is rich and intensively farmed. A little further south, after extensive banana plantations have given way to an arid and eroded landscape, lie the northernmost shores of the Dead Sea. By now, just one hour's drive from the capital, the temperature is a good 19 degrees Fahrenheit (10 degrees Celsius) warmer than it is in Amman and the surrounding hills.

Jordanians love picnics and the temperature difference makes the seashore a popular picnic site in winter, when temperatures in the north plunge surprisingly low and there is at least one deep snowfall every year. Here, at 1,290 feet (393 meters) below sea level, there are no villages. There are only the tents of the Bedouin (wandering Arabs who move their homes with the seasons) and a government resthouse with a restaurant, changing-rooms and private beach area. Rides on the Bedouins' gaily-decorated camels are a visitor's treat but the two pleasure-boats which used to carry tourists lie beached on the shore, abandoned since the 1967 war.

The Dead Sea is one of the earth's oddest environments. Its high salt content (thirty percent) gives the water a slightly soapy feel and makes it impossible for even the non-swimmer to sink. It is great fun to float in but it holds a nasty shock for the swimmer who splashes water into eyes or mouth. The bitter, brackish taste lingers for hours. When bathers dry off in the sun afterwards, the evaporating water leaves a white crust of salt crystals. The many hot freshwater springs which feed the Dead Sea are pleasant places in which to rinse off the salt.

No life can survive in these acrid waters—there are no plants and no fish, and therefore very few birds. A sixth century map of Palestine, made of mosaic and preserved in a church in Madaba (a Christian town south of Amman), shows fish swimming in the Jordan River but turning back at the Dead Sea. The Sea is actually getting saltier by the year as its waters evaporate in a climate where summer temperatures regularly exceed 104 degrees Fahrenheit (40 degrees Celsius).

One of the hot, freshwater springs, which feed the Dead Sea.

Climbing back to Amman, another road passes up through the beautiful Wadi Shuaib. A *wadi* is a river which runs only after the rains have fallen; the word is also used to describe the river's valley. Wadi Shuaib is a green streambed filled with oleander bushes whose pink flowers make a striking contrast with the barrenness left behind. At the head of the wadi lies the small and picturesque town of Salt. This was the region's capital city until 1921, and the site of its first hospital and first school, at which many of Jordan's leading figures were educated.

Eighteen miles (twenty-nine kilometers) to the east lies the modern capital and, to the north, the rolling green hills of ancient

Wadi Shuaib

Gilead. Most of the East Bank's settled populations have lived here since Biblical times. It is here that the ten cities of the Decapolis—a Roman trade league—were established after the Roman invasion in 64 B.C. Jordan's richest archaeological treasure lies beyond the Zarqa River at the ruined Roman city of Jerash. Passing colonnaded streets, temples and triumphal arches, the road continues to Irbid, Jordan's second city, and on to the Syrian border.

Heading south from Amman, there are three fascinating routes. The ancient King's Highway runs along the fertile rim of the plateau to Kerak via one of Jordan's most spectacular sights—the grey and forbidding canyon of the Wadi Mujib. The *wadi* cuts deep into the plateau, opening out as it reaches the Dead Sea. It was declared a nature reserve as part of King Hussein's fiftieth birthday celebrations.

At Kerak, a Christian town and site of a splendid hilltop Crusader castle, the route divides. The King's Highway continues to Petra—a mysterious ruined city hidden deep in the mountains. Another road drops down into the southern end of the Jordan Valley—the magnificent Wadi Araba which runs south from the Dead Sea along the armistice lines between Jordan and Israel. This is a desert road of mountains closing in on rolling sand dunes. A surprising sight is a small Buddhist temple alone in the waste—a souvenir of the Korean engineers who built the military road.

The third route south is the Desert Highway with its constant traffic of trucks crawling northward from Aqaba on their way to Iraq. It is the more direct route and for most of its length it runs parallel to the railway, passing through the western edge of the

A narrow, twisting road through a Jordanian *wadi*.

Greater Syrian Desert which extends south into the vast emptiness of Saudi Arabia.

Much of the Jordanian desert landscape consists of rolling stony expanses covered with flint and limestone flakes or pierced by basalt outcrops. But to the south lie deep, pinkish sands interrupted by massive rock formations. These form the beautiful and unearthly Wadi Rum—a strange moonlike landscape. It was here that the film *Lawrence of Arabia* was made. (T.E. Lawrence was a British soldier in the First World War. He helped the Arabs in their revolt against the Turks who were then occupying their lands.) Much further north lies Azraq where Lawrence wintered during the Arab Revolt and planned his campaigns. Azraq, an oasis town and the site of the first permanent pool of water for more than 620 miles (1,000 kilometers), stands on the edge of the "black desert"—a dark stretch of lava and basalt terrain with a grim beauty of its own.

The three roads south all converge on Aqaba, Jordan's only outlet to the sea. It is situated on the country's scant stretch of Red Sea coast and is of vital importance to Jordan as a port, as a center for industry and as a tourist center. Aqaba makes a fairly successful job of combining the three activities while, at the same time, conserving the precious natural resources of the Red Sea, where tropical fish swim among coral close to the docks and to a plant processing minerals for fertilizer production.

A portrait of T.E. Lawrence (Lawrence of Arabia) who fought in the Arab Revolt of 1916-18.

3

Amman

Jordan's capital city lies in the hilly north of the country, at about 3,000 feet (900 meters) above sea level. The city is built (like Rome) on seven hills, called *jebels*. It houses its population of 1.5 million inhabitants in a small space—from any of its hills the countryside surrounding the town can be clearly seen. Square white houses, mostly one or two stories high, cover the city slopes and narrow streets zigzag down the steep hillsides.

"Downtown"—the way Jordanians translate their word for the center of Amman—earns its title from its physical position as well as its commercial importance. The bustling shopping center lies in a small hollow cradled by the *jebels* which crowd in on it. Amman cannot boast an ancient *souk* (eastern marketplace) like other Arab towns, but downtown still presents a colorful and bustling scene. Small shops line the streets, their frontages mostly open to the pavement. Some are built in narrow arcades or small indoor markets; and shopkeepers often pile their goods to the ceiling, so that they need ladders to reach the goods on the topmost shelves.

A view of "Downtown" Amman.

Peddlars sell small items—socks, lighters and the like—along the pavements; and barrow-boys offer sticky cakes or *kayk* (sesame-seed bread) for sale. Other "fast foods" are available—*shawarma* (lamb sliced from a spit and rolled in flat Arab bread with salad) or *falafel* (small fried rissoles made from ground, spiced chickpeas and served in a sandwich with sesame paste). Bakers' shops are full of small sticky pastries soaked in honey, piled high on huge display stands. Sometimes *sous*-sellers can be seen. These men carry brass urns full of *sous* (a liquorice drink) on their backs, to be poured into the brass cups hung round their waists.

In the fruit and vegetable market, the season's produce is heaped in stalls. Arabs are careful shoppers and it is usually the men of the family who inspect the produce and make the purchases.

Alongside shops selling radios, cameras, tools and engine parts there are still signs of a more ancient way of life. In the spice shops, open sacks of seeds and grains spill out onto the street; a tent shop sells the narrow lengths of closely-woven goat hair which the Bedouin pin together to construct their tents; tailors, quiltmakers and cobblers work in their shop-windows; in the gold *souk,* customers buy presents or the jewelry which makes up a bride's dowry.

"Downtown" marks not only the center of modern-day Amman but the site of the village from which it grew. The town is mentioned in the Bible as Rabbath-Ammon and it grew further in importance in Roman times. The center of the town was probably

The ruins of the Omayyad Palace on Amman's Citadel Hill.

The restored Roman amphitheater in the center of Amman.

Jebel Qal'a (Citadel Hill) where ancient city walls can still be clearly seen. Amman (then known as Philadelphia) became the seat of a bishop when Christianity spread to the region, but later declined into a small village. In 1878, Circassian refugees (Muslims from Russia) settled there. Photographs from the early twentieth century show little but the ruined Roman amphitheater in an empty valley. The amphitheater, carefully restored, now lies in the heart of the modern city.

When Amman became the kingdom's capital city in 1921, it consisted of nothing more than a few streets and dirt roads. There were only three thousand inhabitants and the *jebels* surrounding the village were covered with fields. There was no tap-water or electricity and the streets were lit with kerosene pressure lamps.

By 1943 the town had thirty thousand inhabitants, a population which was to explode overnight with the influx of refugees from Palestine in 1948. The pattern was repeated in 1967, and the city is still struggling to accommodate its present estimated population of about 1.5 million people. The city's suburbs are characterized by constant building work and the bounds of the city have spread so that it almost encompasses nearby towns.

The steep hills and narrow streets in the center of Amman have

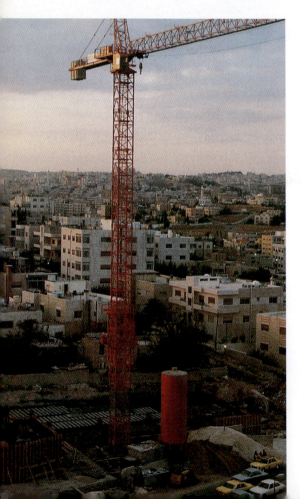

Construction work in Amman—much needed in a city that is struggling to accommodate its present estimated population of about 1.5 million.

The Royal Palace in Amman.

led to a confusion of one-way systems. Maps of the city are complicated by the fact that side streets are often unnamed. Many of the main streets have two or three names—the official name and others more widely-used, based on landmarks or long tradition.

Buses and taxis link the main areas of the city. As well as the private yellow taxis, there are also *servis*-taxis. These are shared taxis. They run along fixed routes, picking up and setting down passengers on the way. *Servis* routes also link one town with another and they are the cheapest way of travelling in Jordan. Drivers often decorate their taxis with an ostrich feather on the bonnet and elaborate cushions, fringes and ornaments inside. Pictures of the Royal Family are popular and good-luck charms or worry-beads (a string of beads used as an aid to prayer) hang from the rear-view mirror.

To the west Amman begins to lose its traditional eastern character. Jebel Amman, the city's most important hill, is characterized by large international hotels, expensive shopping areas, embassies and commercial buildings, as well as the villas of the rich, and increasing numbers of apartments. Here, five- or six-story buildings are not uncommon, in contrast with the eastern hills where small, square, low-lying buildings sit close together in the city's main residential areas.

Jebel Hussein and Wahdat are characterized by two enormous refugee camps, with further camps lying at Baqaa, on the northwestern edge of Amman, and Marka, to the northeast. The camps are almost towns within a town—Baqaa camp has about sixty thousand inhabitants.

A small provincial town thirty years ago, Amman has rapidly acquired all the amenities of a thriving capital. It has a theater complex and conference center, and a major sports center with an Olympic-sized stadium and swimming-pools. There are many movie theaters showing Arabic and western films. The Queen Alia International Airport is about 22 miles (35 kilometers) south of Amman. There is one domestic route between Amman and Aqaba. Main roads are being improved and new highways built.

4

The Region's History

The banks of the Jordan River have been inhabited for at least half a million years. Jericho, on the West Bank, has until recently been considered as the world's oldest surviving settlement. Excavations near by have uncovered a Neolithic (late Stone Age) village built at the beginning of mankind's transition from hunters and gatherers to become farmers and city-dwellers. But recent excavations in Amman itself have revealed a nine-thousand-year-old village at least ten times the size of the Jericho site and including stone and mud-brick houses, human remains, and artifacts such as tools and clay animal figurines.

Remains of other villages show that the region was steadily settled over the next eight thousand years. The pattern of its history was established early as an active international trade developed and the various powers of the region fought over its dominance.

By Biblical times, the region was divided into several kingdoms. The Middle East (the countries of the Eastern

This Byzantine map of Jerusalem is in a church in the Jordanian town of Madaba. The Byzantines came to the Middle East from Constantinople, and were one of the many ancient empires to rule Jordan.

Mediterranean and the Arabian Peninsula) was ruled in turn by a series of ancient empire-builders: the Assyrians, the Babylonians, the Persians and the Macedonians. It was the leader of the Macedonians, Alexander the Great, who introduced Greek culture to the region. Soon Greek became a second language for the educated classes of the area.

Next, the expanding Roman Empire reached the Middle East. The region prospered under Roman rule and, after the conversion of the Emperor Constantine in A.D. 313, Christianity spread quickly in the area. Prosperity continued under the Byzantines, who came from Constantinople to succeed the Romans after their empire collapsed.

Meanwhile, another civilization had been flourishing in the southern city of Petra. The Nabataeans, whose kingdom once stretched as far north as Damascus, controlled the major north-south trade routes from their hidden city.

A new wave of influence came with the advent of the Prophet Muhammad and the establishment of Islam in the seventh century A.D. In 636 the Islamic armies defeated the Byzantine forces at the Battle of Yarmouk. The Byzantines withdrew from the region and Arabic became the language and Islam the religion of the people. At this time the Dome of the Rock and Al-Aqsa mosques—two of the most sacred places of worship for Muslims—were built in Jerusalem.

The ascendancy of Islam prompted the Crusader invasions from Europe. The Crusaders mounted military expeditions in the name of the cross on which Christ died. They wanted to recover the Christian sites in Jerusalem from the Muslim forces who were occupying the Holy Land. They captured the city in 1099 after a terrible siege. The Crusaders then proceeded to consolidate their position in the region and Crusader castles were built at Kerak and Shobak. Their remains can be seen there today.

The Crusaders controlled parts of what is now Jordan until 1187 when a Muslim army under Saladin defeated them at the Battle of Hittin.

The last major external rulers to control the region absolutely were the Ottoman Turks. Their rule began with the conquest of Lebanon, Syria, Jordan, Palestine and Egypt in 1516. The Turks thus controlled the route for Muslim pilgrims travelling from Turkey to the holy sites in Arabia. Apart from this, the area's importance dwindled under Ottoman rule. There was little economic development and the region lost touch with the outside world. At the same time, Turkish influence was weak and the people maintained their Arab identity and culture.

The Ottoman Empire grew weaker during the nineteenth century. By 1914, when the First World War began, Arab nationalists had started to form secret societies which aimed at uniting Arab resistance to the occupiers. They wanted to draw the Arabs together into an independent state and develop the area socially and economically. The Ottoman Empire had allied with Germany, so Britain and her allies in Europe promised to support the Arab cause if the Arab people would rebel against the

The castle of Karak, built by the Christian Crusaders in the twelfth century as a stronghold against their Muslim enemies.

Ottomans. The Arab Revolt of 1916 was the result; and the Turks were overthrown.

However, the Arab nationalists were not told about a secret agreement between Britain and France. The Sykes-Picot Agreement was to divide Arab lands under the authority of the two European powers. The agreement also established the idea of a Jewish homeland in Palestine—a concept which is still being fought over. The Sykes-Picot Agreement placed the Amirate (principality) of Transjordan—the East Bank—under British administration for thirty years after the end of the First World War. This period is known as the British Mandate and marks Jordan's entry into the modern world.

The many peoples who have lived in Jordan and travelled across its lands during its rich history have left a priceless archaeological heritage behind them. In many parts of the kingdom there is no need to dig for history. At ancient sites the ground surface itself is scattered with pieces of mosaic, fragments of broken pottery (shards) and even Stone-Age flint tools. Roman temples and desert castles have lasted well in the dry climate; and experts who have learned to read the surface for signs have uncovered buried towns and villages from all periods of history and prehistory.

The first traces of human life in Jordan have been found in the eastern desert, where archaeologists have discovered flint tools and hand-axes from half a million years ago. It was a road-builder's bulldozer which first uncovered the site of the world's earliest known Neolithic settlement at Ain Ghazal, near the center of Amman.

Successive eras of human occupation all left their traces; often these lie one on top of another. Ideal sites for villages—near water and easy to defend against enemies—were scarce. So when a village was destroyed by fire, earthquake or enemy attack, another group of people might choose to build a second village on the same site. They levelled off the ruins and built directly on top of them and, in time, a *tell* (an artificial city-hill) was formed. Many such *tells* can be seen in modern Jordan; archaeologists have dug through their layers, uncovering remains from many different ages.

The Roman and Nabataean civilizations left Jordan with its two most remarkable tourist attractions. The Romans established the ten cities of the Decapolis, a commercial league which included Amman (then known as Philadelphia).

Where these cities once stood, temples, pillars, amphitheaters and baths now remain. Jerash (ancient Gerasa), in particular, has survived the years intact, and intensive archaeological work has led to the reconstruction of many of its splendors. Jerash's cobbled and colonnaded main street connects the forum (meeting-place) with the Temple of Artemis. A triumphal arch marks the southern entrance of the city, which boasts two amphitheaters (semi-circular open-air theaters) and a hippodrome (race-course), as well as public baths, temples and churches.

Nabataean culture left its major monument in the hidden city of Petra. Petra lies deep in the mountains of southern Jordan and, although historians knew of its existence, it was not until 1812 that a Swiss explorer (named Jean Louis Burckhardt)

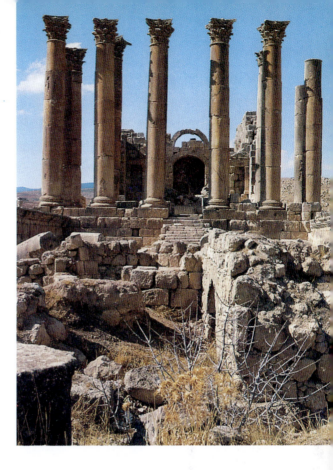

The Temple of Artemis, Jerash.

rediscovered it. Some years later, Dean Burgon (a nineteenth century clergyman) made the ruins famous with a prize-winning poem in which he called Petra "a rose-red city half as old as Time." Visitors used to reach the city on horseback or on foot, but now JETT (Air-con Jordan Express Tourism Transport) provides minibus service to the city everyday. The treasury, like many buildings in Petra, is cut into the mountainside, with its magnificent facade carved from the rock itself. The Bedouin who live in Petra's caves believe that Moses hid his treasure in the carved urn which tops the treasury. Bullet holes scar the facade where they have shot at the urn in the hope of releasing its gold.

The Jordan government's Department of Antiquities was set up in 1924 to direct archaeological research in what was then Transjordan. Today it is active in salvaging sites threatened by modern development and in organizing emergency excavations. The department encourages foreign teams to undertake digs and restoration schemes. Jordan's universities have their own archaeological departments. American and European archaeological institutes also have bases in Amman.

The Nabataean city of Petra, hidden deep in the mountains of southern Jordan. It can only be reached on horseback or on foot.

5

The History of the Modern Kingdom

With the establishment of the British Mandate, the throne of Transjordan (the new name given to the lands on the East Bank of the Jordan River) went to Abdullah, son of the Arab nationalist leader Sherif Hussein.

By 1923 the British had recognized Transjordan as a state preparing for independence and, on May 25, 1946, the country was declared a kingdom and became an independent state under its modern name: the Hashemite Kingdom of Jordan (the term "Hashemite" is taken from the family name of the King). The new kingdom took the colors of the Arab Revolt for its flag—it is black, white, green and red with a white seven-pointed star in the hoist (the inner edge).

The young country faced immediate and severe problems with the turmoil in neighboring Palestine which followed the Second World War (1939-1945), the attempts to establish a Jewish homeland there and British withdrawal from the region.

In 1948, after the proclamation of the State of Israel, Arab armies entered Palestine. The Arab Legion (a reserve force of local troops formed in Transjordan by Frederick Peake, a British officer) retained control of parts of East Jerusalem and the most important Muslim shrines. But by the end of the year only the Gaza Strip, East Jerusalem and the West Bank remained under Arab control and half a million Palestinians had fled to Jordan. The kingdom's population doubled and the United Nations Organization set up its Relief and Works Agency (UNRWA) to help the refugees. Camps were set up to house the influx of Palestinians.

The West and East Bank areas merged in 1950 with the formal annexation of the West Bank by a newly-elected Jordanian parliament made up of representatives from both sides of the river.

In 1951, King Abdullah of Jordan was assassinated as he went to Friday prayers at the Al-Aqsa Mosque in Jerusalem. His grandson, Hussein, saw the killing. A bullet fired at the young boy rebounded from a medal he was wearing. It has been said that the assassination was part of a plot formed by Palestinians worried about the king's motives in the newly-annexed West Bank, where he had been strengthening the security forces, and angered by his negotiations with Israel for a peace treaty. Abdullah was succeeded by his son Talal but one month later the new king was forced to abdicate through illness. The young Hussein, still a pupil at Harrow School in England, became king.

The young ruler inherited many problems. Not only was his kingdom struggling to cope with the doubling of its population, but

Palestinian guerrillas were attacking Israel from Jordan, inciting heavy Israeli retaliation.

Tensions culminated in a second Arab war with Israel in 1967. Israel seized the West Bank and, at a stroke, the Jordan Valley lost almost its entire population as 200,000 refugees fled from the West to the East Bank.

The years following the 1967 war were difficult. With a war-damaged economy the country had to house further hundreds of thousands of refugees. More problems followed and, in 1971, a ten-day civil war was fought in the streets of Amman between the Jordanian army and Palestinian guerrillas. The Jordanian forces kept control. Palestinian refugees were given full status as Jordanian citizens, provided they accepted the rule of government.

6

Government

King Hussein bin Talal came to power in 1953 and has stayed there ever since. A much-loved leader and formidable statesman, Hussein was born in 1935 and educated in Jordan, Egypt and Britain. His father, King Talal, was forced to abdicate through ill-health while Hussein was still at school. Hussein assumed the throne in 1953 at the age of eighteen. His present wife, Queen Noor, is American born. His brother, Crown Prince Hassan, is King Hussein's heir and acts as regent during the king's frequent absences from the country on affairs of state. King Hussein plays a key role, not only in the government of his own country but in Middle Eastern affairs as a whole, and in international politics.

The independent Hashemite Kingdom dates from May 25, 1946. The constitution was published in February 1947, and the first elections were held in October of the same year.

The constitution gives the king wide-ranging powers. He appoints the prime minister and members of the Cabinet as well as the Senate, or upper house of Parliament. The lower house of

King Hussein of Jordan. This photograph was taken during an official visit to the United States.

Parliament is elected by the people. Men and women who are over the age of twenty are allowed to vote in general elections. The present House of Deputies (the lower house) has eighty members.

Jordan is divided into eight districts, called *muhafazahs* (wards), each named after the chief of the district in question. *Muhafazahs* are sub-divided and local government is organized through municipalities, village councils, or village headmen.

The north, south and central Bedouin each have a representative in Parliament to speak for their special interests. The Desert Patrol was formed in 1931 by the Amir Abdullah, in order to put an end to tribal feuding. Now the patrolmen help in the administration of the Bedouin as well as policing the desert. They still use camels and

A member of Jordan's Desert Patrol in his colorful uniform.

wear a colorful uniform—long khaki tunics and red *keyfiyahs* (headcloths), with red leather belts, brass insignia and silver daggers.

The roots of the Jordanian army lie in the Arab Revolt of 1916. Soldiers who took part in the rebellion joined the Arab Legion under Peake Pasha. The Legion developed under Sir John Glubb, an Englishman who stayed on after independence until King Hussein relieved him of his command when he decided to Arabize the armed forces in 1956. Today, Jordan has a modern army and air force, with a small naval base at Aqaba. Male Jordanians undertake two years of compulsory national service in either the armed forces, the police or the civil defence.

The law in Jordan is administered through the civil courts and the religious courts. The religious (*Sharia*) courts deal with religious affairs and with personal law for Muslims—matters such as marriage, divorce and inheritance. The Sharia courts also decide on affairs involving any religious charitable endowment. Non-Muslims have recourse to the Religious Community Councils.

Religious and public life in Jordan are closely integrated. There is a Ministry of Awqaf and Islamic Affairs. *Awqaf* are charities which have been set up to run mosques, cemeteries, schools and other institutions.

7

The People

The land that is now Jordan has always supported two distinct ways of life. The nomadic tribes who wandered over the desert and established tribal territories in the region are the ancestors of the modern Bedouin who now make up seven percent of the kingdom's population. But settled town life is nothing new to the region and has been the pattern of life in the West Bank and the western edge of the East Bank for thousands of years.

The desert Bedouin were traditionally the camel-breeders. Each extended family claimed allegiance to one of the many tribes of Jordan, recognizing the tribal leader (*sheikh*) and fighting together against the enemies of the tribe. Living in goat-hair tents, they roamed the desert in search of water and grazing for their herds. At the same time they benefitted from their animals' milk, meat and skins, and even from their dung which was burned as fuel in a treeless environment.

They moved their herds deep into the desert with the news of the year's first rains after the long dry season and returned to the edge of the desert for the dry summer months. This was the time for buying and selling in the towns and also for terrorizing farming communities by demanding protection money. This fee would buy the "protection" of one Bedouin tribe against the raids of other tribes.

Shepherd tribes, tending flocks of sheep and goats, lived on the desert fringes, between the cultivated areas and the dry desert interior. These Bedouin led a more settled life, pitching their tents in temporary "villages." Part of the year might be spent in the search for good pasture but in the wetter months the family might settle near plentiful grazing land and even try to grow a few crops.

Today, some Bedouin still follow the traditional way of life. They live with few tools and no furniture, carrying their homes on the backs of their camels when the desert's scanty pasture is exhausted and new grazing has to be found. The Bedouin are superb animal farmers. They are the only people who know the secrets of the desert: where to find water and how to survive in the harsh terrain which makes up most of Jordan's territory.

But for most of the Bedouin living in Jordan today, life is changing. They are a fighting race and their service in Jordan's modern army has brought them into contact with a different way of life. Their hunger for education has meant that families need to spend at least part of the year settled close to a school. Overgrazing of available pasture has also forced change and now the government is involved in the adjustment from a nomadic life to permanent settlement. In some areas, the Ministry of

A Bedouin tent in Wadi Rum.

Agriculture provides training in farming techniques. Elsewhere, families have been given land, and the government has built schools and clinics. Near the ancient ruined city of Petra, where generations of Bedouin have made their homes in caves, the government has built a new village to rehouse them.

The Bedouin are a small sector of Jordanian society but their influence is enormous. Traditional desert values have become central to Jordanian culture. Bravery, honor and loyalty are prized above all other virtues. King Hussein himself comes from Bedouin stock and is a popular figure among the tribes, who have always been stalwart supporters of the monarchy. It was Bedouin backing which helped save the king when some sections of the army moved against him in an uprising in 1957.

Hospitality is the single virtue most notably connected with the

Bedouin and, by extension, with all Arabs. For people living alone in the desert, the arrival of a stranger meant valuable news and contact with the wider world. It would be unthinkable to allow a traveller to pass by without observing the rituals of hospitality—the honor of the tribe would suffer irreparable damage if the proper treatment was not given to a guest.

In a world where the Bedouin owned practically nothing, it was an act of great bravery as well as generosity for a family to share what little it had with a guest. The head of the family would slaughter an animal in honor of the stranger and, although this might be the only time they would taste meat, no one would eat before the guest had finished. Dark, strong Bedouin coffee would be served, and other rituals of welcome scrupulously observed. Once the guest had eaten, rested and taken his departure, he would remain under his host's protection for a

A Bedouin child near Petra.

The cave dwelling of one of the last remaining Bedouin families in Petra.

further three days. The host and his family would avenge him if anybody harmed him.

Jordan's present-day population of nearly five million is partly a result of immigration. The first of the refugees who were to swell the region's population were the Circassians—Muslim tribespeople who emigrated from the Caucasus after its conquest by the Russians in the last century. With them came a smaller group of Chechens, another Muslim tribe. These groups still cherish their own culture. The king's personal bodyguard, made up of Circassians, is a splendid sight in dark costumes and bandoliers.

But by far the biggest impact on Jordan's population came with the two massive waves of Palestinian refugees following successive struggles with Israel. Today, there are approximately 1.3 million

Palestinians living in Jordan—about one-third of the population. Thirty-one percent still live in refugee camps. There are ten camps in the country. The original tents have been replaced by rough mud-brick or concrete shelters. A typical shelter consists of two rooms, a cooking area and a courtyard. Narrow pathways and dusty streets run between these homes. The camps are very overcrowded and some still have no electricity or running water. Drainage is usually by means of a system of open ditches. Life is hard. But many people (those who have not been able to recover financially from the loss of their homes and all their possessions) have nowhere else to go. Other refugees remain through choice, reluctant to settle permanently in a new country, and insisting on their right to return to their homes in what was once Palestine.

UNRWA—the United Nations Relief and Works Agency—looks after the refugees. UNRWA staff help the residents organize the camp, create employment, distribute basic food rations to the neediest, and run welfare services and schools.

Most Palestinians—the remaining sixty percent—now live on their own, outside the camps. They live on the same terms as other citizens, playing an important role in the life of the country. Many play a key part in government and in business life.

8

The Year

Jordan runs on two calendars. The official calendar follows the 365-day year used in the western world; but religious matters depend on the Islamic calendar.

The Islamic calendar is calculated from A.D. 622. Years are numbered from 0 A.H. (Anno Hegirae), the year of the *Hijrah* when the Prophet Muhammad and his followers migrated from hostile Mecca. He and his community were suffering persecution in the town, so they fled to Medina. There are twelve months in the Islamic calendar and each month has twenty-nine or thirty days, making the Muslim year ten days shorter than the western year. Religious festivals naturally follow this calendar and their timing depends on the first sighting of the new moon. This means that the date of important festivals often remains uncertain until just a few days beforehand.

The Islamic year revolves around the holy month of Ramadan. Ramadan begins with the first sighting of the new moon and, for thirty days, Muslims must fast between daybreak

Muslims praying amidst the ruins of Jerash.

and sunset. Eating, drinking and smoking are forbidden during the daylight hours. The sale of alcohol (normally permitted in Jordan) is forbidden during Ramadan and bars are closed. The atmosphere in the streets is subdued, and shops and offices close early. But after the sun goes down the atmosphere changes and there are nightly feasts for family and friends.

Two major festivals follow Ramadan. The first, Eid al-Fitr (the Feast of the Breaking of the Fast) celebrates the end of the holy month. The second, Eid al-Adha (the Feast of Sacrifice) marks the end of the pilgrimage season.

The Five Pillars of Islam—duties of every Muslim—are the profession of faith ("There is no God but Allah and Muhammad

53

is his prophet"), prayer, alms-giving (charity), fasting during the holy month, and the *hajj* or pilgrimage to Mecca. Once in a lifetime, every Muslim who can afford it should visit the holy city and offer a sacrifice.

Not all Jordanians are Muslims. There is a sizeable Christian minority, so Christian festivals also mark the passing of the year. Religious freedom is written into the kingdom's constitution. The approach of Christmas and Easter are signalled by the arrival of seasonal decorations in the shops.

The western New Year (January 1) is celebrated enthusiastically. Other important bank holidays are Labor Day (May 1), Jordan Independence and Army Day (May 25), the anniversary of King Hussein's accession to the throne (August 11) and the King's Birthday (November 14).

January and February are the coldest months of the year. There are often heavy snowfalls in the capital and the hilly north. Bitterly cold winds and rainstorms, with the danger of sudden floods, can make the weather really miserable at this time of the year. But bad weather is interspersed with bright sunny weeks and, if things get too bad, there is always the valley or the warmer south to escape to.

Spring comes with March and April. It is a beautiful season in Jordan. Fields and hills—which a few months before looked bare and scorched—become green. Flowers bloom everywhere in variety and great profusion. Poppies and dark red anemones cover the fields, and every verge is filled with delicately colored wild flowers. The eucalyptus trees put out yellow balls of pollen and later the oleander bushes along each dried-up wadi will be covered in pink blossoms. Even in the desert, flowers appear from nowhere, the most striking of them all being the rare black iris.

By May, the long summer has set in. Temperatures in Jordan never become unbearably hot. The worst feature of the summer climate is the *khamsin*—a period of oppressive and dusty heat lasting for several weeks at a time.

The major national event of the summer months is the Jerash Festival. Started in 1981, this festival of culture and arts has for its magnificent setting the ruined Roman city of Jerash. The city's two amphitheaters host celebrated dance and drama companies from the Arab world and beyond, as well as internationally-respected musicians. The old Roman streets are lined with local craftsmen demonstrating their skills, as well as with *falafel* and *shawarma* stands and smaller temporary platforms for overspill performances. Every night for two weeks the floodlit cobbles and colonnades are thronged with people.

Midsummer marks the annual return of many expatriate Jordanians. Working in Saudi Arabia and the countries of the Persian Gulf, where wages are high and educated personnel are much in demand, they return every year to visit their families and homes. So many Jordanians work abroad that their numbers make a noticeable difference to the population.

After the long summer of continuous sunshine and drought, the first chills of autumn come as some relief. People begin to look forward to the first rainfall which, if it comes too late, may

The restored southern amphitheater at Jerash. Every summer this is the setting for a festival of culture and the arts.

ruin next year's farming. Prayers are said in the mosques. Winter proper sets in about December. During the winter months, the northern hills expect around 16 inches (41 centimeters) of rainfall, but the desert areas normally receive less than 2 inches (5 centimeters).

9

Family Life and Daily Routines

Home and family life are central to the Arab way of life. Families in Jordan are large and very few people live alone. Even students and young adults usually live in the family home until they marry.

Traditionally, families of ten or more children were the rule and today they are by no means uncommon. Moreover, the Arab family often includes more than just parents and children. A man's children, grandchildren and brothers with their families may all live in the same house or in houses built close together. Close connections are kept up among the extended family of cousins reaching to many removes. Property is owned communally by the family, whose members all work in the family business or on the same farm.

In the cities, smaller families living separately are becoming more common but the wider family is still of the first importance. Social life turns on the family circle, with much visiting between relatives and big family parties for any celebration.

Marriage is considered the normal state and very few Jordanians remain unmarried. Most couples meet through the family circle. Sometimes marriages are arranged by the parents, although the final decision to marry will be made by the couple themselves. Women who marry leave their own family and become absorbed by their husband's family. Property they inherit is lost to their own family and this is one reason why marriages between cousins are still quite common.

Marriage within the family has other advantages—parents will know the suitor and he is likely to come from a similar background and have similar interests.

Couples have two engagement ceremonies. The unofficial engagement is when they announce their decision to family and friends. The formal engagement is a serious affair—the actual marriage contract is often signed at this stage. This contract can only be broken by divorce, even though the actual marriage has not yet taken place. The contract records the couple's consent to marry and includes the bride-price to be paid by the groom. Part of the money is used by the bride for clothes and household equipment. The rest will be her security against widowhood or divorce. The bride money required by many families for their daughters can run into huge sums and many young men have to delay marriage for some years before they have saved enough to meet the price of a bride.

The engagement and the marriage itself are marked by big parties. The bride is given presents of gold jewelry. (The gold which Jordanian women are given throughout their life represents a safe investment for them and one which can easily be turned into cash if necessary.)

Islam permits a man to take as many as four wives, provided he can afford to do so and gives each wife equal care and attention. This custom, never common in Jordan, is now almost unheard of.

Arabs love children and rarely wait long before starting a family. The birth of the first child causes great delight, especially if it is a boy. Parents are often referred to by the name of their eldest son. If the boy is called Ahmad, the parents become Abu Ahmad (father of Ahmad) and Um Ahmad (mother of Ahmad). In Muslim families, circumcision is the first important event in a boy's life and the occasion of a family celebration. For Christians, baptism is of equal importance.

Children in Wadi Rum. Arabs love children, and large families (with up to ten children) are common in Jordan.

The ordinary working day starts early for Jordanian families. Business hours start at 8:00 a.m. and schools also open early. The working week is six days long, running from Saturday to Thursday, but the office day is short. Offices close in time for a late lunch or, if work continues until 6:00 p.m., employees have long lunch-breaks. Shops usually open at around 8:00 a.m. and do not close until quite late at night. Away from the town centers, however, shopkeepers put up their shutters for most of the afternoon, re-opening at around 3:00 or 4:00 p.m.

Breakfast in a Jordanian household is a small meal. Most people eat flat Arab *pitta* bread with *hummus* (pureed chickpeas). Or the bread may be served with yogurt, or dipped in olive oil and a mixture of spices called *zatar*.

The main meal of the day is at lunchtime. It might be stuffed vegetables (a Middle Eastern specialty) or some form of lamb casserole with rice. The meal will be served with a range of Arab salads (*mezze*) and with *pitta*.

Supper is usually a simple meal of bread and salads, with leftovers from lunchtime. Desserts are simple—fresh fruit or local pastries are what is usually served.

Friday is the week's holy day for Muslims and the weekend holiday in Jordan. Men and boys go to the mosque (the Muslim place of worship) for the Friday prayers and sermon. These are also broadcast from the minaret (the tower from which the call to prayer issues five times a day). Women pray at home—they never go to the mosque. Christian services are held on Sundays. In

A Jordanian mosque—the calls to prayer, five times each day, are issued from the top of the slender minaret.

Jordan this is the middle of the working week, so Christians are allowed to take a few hours off in order to attend church.

Friday is also the day for going visiting, and for a special meal with family and friends. And it is the day for picnics—a popular Jordanian pastime. There are many beautiful picnic sites in the country. The ideal spot has a shady tree with a stream nearby. Picnics are elaborate affairs. Whole meals are cooked on simple portable barbecues and shared among the guests.

Jordanians take pride in their reputation for hospitality and many occasions are made into an excuse for a celebration. Parties are characterized by enormous and splendid arrays of food. Women ask their sisters and friends to help with the preparations because Arab cuisine is elaborate and many dishes take hours to prepare. Carefully-stuffed vegetables and beautifully-garnished plates of *mezze* may be offered, but the pride of festive cookery is the *mensaf*.

This is a Bedouin dish now offered in all Jordanian houses as a great honor to the guest. It consists of mutton cooked with yogurt sauce, served on enormous platters of rice and pine nuts, atop a base of thin bread. The guests eat from the communal dish, using their right hands only to make a small ball of rice, sauce and a morsel of meat, and flicking the food into their mouths with their thumbs. Although a visit from a stranger may have been the only time many of the Bedouin would have tasted meat, neither the host nor his family would eat until the guest had finished.

Celebrations of any kind also involve music, singing and dancing. Women and men often gather for separate parties in different rooms. Women may do belly dances. For men there is the *dubke*: dancers line up side by side with their arms around each other's shoulders, following steps performed by the leader. Children are to be seen forming their own line and copying the adults.

10

Village Life and Agriculture

While Amman grows rapidly and its population becomes increasingly westernized, in Jordan's villages life continues much as it has always done.

There have always been villages in Jordan and the villagers were probably farming their land before the Bedouin appeared. Jordanian villages today have hardly changed in appearance since Bible times. The houses are small and built close together. Each dwelling has its small courtyard, surrounded by a wall. Two-story houses are rare and often have outside staircases. Once the buildings were made of mud, rough-cut stone or grey adobe (sun-dried) brick. These can still be seen but now, although the style of construction is little changed, concrete is taking over as the main construction material.

Villages are not characterized by any large or special building. The mosque, although an important center, is usually as small as the houses surrounding it. Other central buildings include small shops and the government school.

A typical Jordanian village, just off the King's Highway.

Most of the people in any village will probably be related, and family ties are strong. Families may have a communal guesthouse which the men use as a meeting-place and club.

Most country people wear the traditional clothes of the area. For the men, this means ankle-length gowns or loose trousers in plain, dark colors. They wear headcloths called *keyfiyahs*, or *hatta* in the local dialect. These are made of a square of material folded in half diagonally and held in place with an *agal*, or black head-rope. *Keyfiyahs* are usually made of light white cotton for the summer and of a warmer material, checked in red or black, for the winter. In the cold winter months, men wear sheepskin-lined cloaks of dark blue, black or brown wool, trimmed with black braid.

Women wear long belted dresses, usually in dark colors. The bodice, hem and side panels, however, are closely embroidered in bright silks. The patterns used vary from village to village and they often have a symbolic meaning. Traditional headgear was once more elaborate, but now most women wear a large scarf of plain white cotton for everyday use. They tie two corners under the chin, leaving most of the material to hang down at the back.

Almost all Jordan's villagers make their living from the land, but a larger village may also support a coffeehouse owner or

A Jordanian man in traditional dress.

Muslim women in Amman.

shopkeeper, a cobbler, a carpenter and possibly even a blacksmith. An important figure is the religious leader—the *immam*—whose role combines the jobs of prayer-leader, preacher and religious teacher. The village is led by its *mukhtar*, or much-respected headman, who is helped by the village council. The headman is elected by the people and paid a salary by the government. He acts as the official link between central government and the village. His job includes the relaying of government instructions, registration of births, deaths and marriages and the welcoming of guests.

Surrounding the village are its fields. Boundaries are not marked with fences; instead, small piles of stones mark the limits of each man's property. In the highlands, farming depends on the annual rainfall. Yields vary dramatically from year to year according to the quantity of rain which fell the previous winter. Wheat and barley are the major crops. Where the land is too hilly for grains, fruit trees are planted in terraces cut into the hillside. Olives, grapes and pistachio nuts are important products.

More important still is the fruit and vegetable production in the Jordan Valley. Here, a series of major irrigation schemes have made much more intensive farming possible and the valley stays green when higher, cooler ground is brown and dusty. Chief among the crops grown are tomatoes, grapes, cucumbers, oranges, lemons and melons, with a whole range of other fruit and vegetables besides.

Experiments with farming on land reclaimed from the desert have proved encouraging. Although the desert is dry, water lies below the surface and this can be used for irrigation. Several agricultural schemes have been set up, including one at Al-Jafr in the southern desert, where 2,450 *dunums* are now flourishing. (A *dunum* is the Jordanian measure of land: one *dunum* is 1,200 square yards or 1,000 square meters.) Another farming experiment is looking at the possibility of using waste water (discharged by houses and factories) for irrigation.

Cows, which need high-quality grazing land, are a rare sight anywhere in Jordan; most of the milk drunk in the kingdom is

An experimental agricultural center in Wadi Araba.

imported as dried milk powder. Pigs are not kept at all because Muslims regard them as unclean animals and the Koran forbids the consumption of pork. Sheep and goats, on the other hand, graze everywhere in Jordan. It is not uncommon even in Amman itself to see a shepherd carefully herding his flock across a busy two-lane highway to exercise his family's ancient grazing rights on some small patch of land still undeveloped. Flocks manage to survive on the most barren-looking land. Goats will even stand on their hind legs to reach the leafy lower branches of trees. The Bedouin manage to graze huge flocks in the desert, where herds of camels also survive on the scrubby vegetation. Animal husbandry is usually the main source of livelihood for the nomadic people. In fact, overgrazing, especially by goats which are undiscriminating feeders, has been a major problem in Jordan and one which is only now being brought under control.

Agricultural methods and machinery in use vary widely across the country. Some farmers, aided by government and private investment, are able to benefit from the most modern equipment and techniques. In other areas, plowing by hand is still a common sight, with plows drawn by horse or bullock. Sowing and reaping are also still done by hand as they were in Bible times. Donkeys were the traditional beasts of burden in Jordan and are still widely used for carrying water, crops and people. The farmer's whole family is likely to have to work in the fields at busy times

A Jordanian shepherd with his flock.

New woodlands between Amman and Jerash.

of the year. Even the smallest children make themselves useful by guarding sheep and goats, or selling produce by the wayside.

Jordan was once a heavily-wooded country but the Turks cut almost all the timber and used it to make sleepers and provide fuel for the Hejaz railway. Now concentrated efforts are being made to replace the forests by tree-planting projects and public campaigns. There is even an annual tree-planting day. The new woodlands will not only provide badly-needed timber but will help prevent soil from being eroded by the action of wind and rain.

11

Traditional Crafts

Before industry on a modern scale was established in Jordan, people made what they needed at home or bought it from local craftsmen. Now that factory-made items are cheaply available, the ancient crafts are continued for their decorative qualities and for their appeal to the tourist trade.

Spinning and weaving have always been important. It is still possible to see country women tending flocks while spinning their wool on a hand-held distaff. Bedouin women weave on large but simple ground-looms—huge frames laid out on the ground. The looms are narrow but very long. Lengths of woven goat hair are pinned together to make tent-coverings or sewn into rugs and camel trappings. Tents are normally black with some white hair woven into the material but rugs include bands of color or are woven in simple stripes.

The center of village weaving is Madaba, a Christian town twenty miles (thirty-three kilometers) south of Amman on the King's Highway. Here, where weavers have worked since 400 B.C., simple mechanical looms are used in workshops where three days' labor makes a classic Madaba rug. These are made from local sheep's wool mixed with goat hair. Natural dyes once produced the traditional colors—deep reds and blues. Nowadays, chemical dyes are more widely used to make bright geometrical designs in browns, greens and oranges.

Straw and bamboo leaves are used in another form of weaving. They are plaited into mats and baskets which are then decorated in muted colors.

A hand-woven rug from Madaba.

Hand-painted Jordanian pottery.

Embroidery is a skill much practiced today and still used for its traditional purpose. Local women wear long gowns with patterned bodices. These are richly decorated with closely-worked cross-stitch which completely covers the front of the dress as well as the hem and side-panels.

Each village has its own characteristic costume and traditional embroidery designs. To do the embroidery, the women first overlay the cloth for their dress with a soft, fine canvas. The threads of the canvas make guidelines for the embroidery stitches. These are sewn in bright colors through the cloth and canvas. When the embroidery is finished, the canvas threads are gently pulled out, leaving the beautifully-worked cloth behind.

Nowadays, the same embroidery technique is used to decorate cushion covers, wallhangings and small souvenirs for sale. Several organizations run workshops and projects which give employment to refugee women and help keep alive the old skills.

Men's winter cloaks are lined with sheepskin. Jordanian sheep have long, silky wool. Sheepskins are also used to make rugs, slippers and western-style clothes, such as jackets and coats.

Handmade glass and ceramics are also still produced today. Handblown glass is made in Amman (and in Hebron, in the West Bank). Blue, green, brown and turquoise are the traditional colors for glass. Jerusalem pottery is painted with brightly-colored floral designs on a white background. Huge pots of rough earthenware are on sale at stalls set up beside the main roads. These pots are meant for storing water, but they are not watertight. If they were, the water inside would soon get hot in the warmth of the sun. But, because they are porous, the water seeping through their sides evaporates, keeping the inside temperature low and the remaining water cool.

Jordan's other crafts are more purely ornamental. The West Bank produces olive-wood carvings and goods made from mother-of-pearl. The olive wood is locally grown. The mother-of-pearl used to come from the Red Sea but now it is imported. These two materials are used to make nativity scenes and models of the Al-Aqsa Mosque in Jerusalem, as well as ornamental boxes, mirrors, picture frames and jewelry.

Bedu jewelry is still being made and worn by the Bedouin and by the village women. Dull silver is wrought into heavy bracelets, rings and necklaces and decorated with lucky stones—cornelians, coral, amber and blue malachite, symbolizing love, good health, success and protection from the evil eye.

One Bedouin tribe still produces beautiful swords and daggers, sheathed in richly ornamented cases.

The colored sands of Petra, Wadi Rum and Aqaba, along with artificially-dyed sands, are used to make sand-bottles. The craftsman pours the sand carefully into the bottle through a tiny funnel and works it with special tools to form colored layers, incorporating flowers, birds and even the Jordanian flag. The bottle-tops betray the origin of the bottles—they are often miniature gin and whisky bottles and sometimes even old soft drink bottles!

Active trade throughout the Arab world has always brought Jordan into contact with craftsmen from other regions. In particular, Damascus (the capital of Syria) has always had a sophisticated crafts industry, supplying Jordan with silk, inlay, and brass and copper work.

As Jordan becomes increasingly westernized through greater contact with the wider world, Jordanians are becoming more and more aware of their valuable cultural heritage. Two museums—in the east and west wings of Amman's Roman Amphitheater—display costumes, jewelry, everyday objects and

Making sand-bottles with colored sand.

tableaux of life as it was once lived in Jordan. Some private citizens are also building up valuable collections of Jordanian crafts. The Jordan Crafts Center in Amman aims to encourage production today by providing the country's best craftsmen with a market for their work.

12

Industry, Communications and the Economy

Jordan is a country with few natural resources. Much of its land is infertile or too dry for farming. Its population is small. The country has hardly any sources of raw materials or fuel to feed and run factories. Drought is a constant threat. It has always been a struggle to produce enough food for the people and to find enough water for their needs. What is more, the country has had to fight for its survival on several occasions in the few decades since its independence, and wars in the Middle East have at times stretched its reserves to the limit.

Until recent years, farming was the country's only livelihood. People barely produced enough for their own needs and commerce on a modern scale hardly existed. But since its independence the Hashemite Kingdom has put huge efforts into the formation of a modern economy—efforts which are now beginning to pay off.

Jordan, unlike its far richer neighbors, is not an oil-producing country. Prospectors searching the country to map its mineral resources have drilled test-holes in the northeastern desert and discovered small amounts of oil which has inspired the government in its search, but so far results are not very encouraging.

The country does, however, have other mineral wealth. Most important is the phosphate, found all over the country and mined near Amman and in the southern desert. Phosphate rock is valuable for use in making fertilizers, and in the chemical industry generally. Jordan is one of the world's largest producers of phosphate. The rock is mined using open-cast techniques—the ore is dug from the surface, not from deep under the ground. The Jordan Fertilizer Industry Company has built a plant south of the port at Aqaba, where the valuable ore is processed.

Potash (potassium chloride) is also used in fertilizer production. Potash is found in quantity in the mineral-rich waters of the Dead Sea. The Arab Potash Company has built a huge refinery at the southern end of the Sea. Evaporation ponds now stretch out across the water. The heat of the sun is enough to evaporate the water, leaving the minerals behind.

Jordan also quarries its own gravel and marble (a favorite building material), and produces cement, which finds a ready market with the country's flourishing building industry.

As Jordan does not produce its own oil, it imports crude (oil in its natural state). The Jordan Petroleum Refinery company processes the oil. All Jordan's gasoline and other petroleum fuels are produced by this company.

A potash plant at Aqaba.

Apart from these major plants, Jordan is not a country of large factories and sprawling industrial regions. There are, however, many small and medium-sized factories engaged in light industry. These are mainly centered in Amman and its surroundings, especially in the area between Amman and Zarqa, fourteen miles (twenty-three kilometers) to the northeast. Products made locally include pharmaceuticals (medicines); food, drink and tobacco; clothing; paper and cardboard; plastics; detergents; and paints.

Water and fuel, vital for industry, are both scarce and expensive in Jordan. The country's development plans concentrate on careful management of these resources. Water is pumped from the second longest river, the Yarmouk River; from the Azraq oasis in the eastern desert; and from wells sunk to

79

water-bearing rocks beneath the surface. The King Talal Dam, in the hill country north of Amman, has created a huge reservoir. Other schemes which have been in the planning stage for some years include a long pipeline from the Euphrates River in Iraq and a huge dam at Maqarin on the Yarmouk River. The dam would not only go a long way to meet Jordan's demands for water, it would also provide much-needed hydro-electric power.

A major problem which has handicapped Jordan's commercial development has been its poor transport and communications services. When King Hussein ascended the throne in 1953, hardly any of the roads in his kingdom were surfaced. Aqaba, the country's only outlet to the sea, was nothing but a small village on a sandy bay. The Hejaz Railway stopped thirty-one miles (fifty kilometers) north of the sea. The Royal Jordanian Airline, Alia, which means "high," was formed in 1962 but the country's major international airport did not open until 1983. The telephone system was elementary and Amman's single radio station had such a limited range that most of the country could not receive its programs.

The country's planners have made great strides in overcoming these problems. Now the kingdom's towns and cities are linked by reasonable roads, with twenty-two miles (thirty-five kilometers) of paved highway linking the airport with the capital. Aqaba has developed beyond recognition and is now a thriving town and tourist center, and a vital import and transit terminus,

A dam between Amman and Jerash.

not only for Jordan but also for neighboring Syria and Iraq. The traffic of goods exported from and imported to these countries provides Jordan with an important source of income.

Busy traffic to and from the port has, however, brought its own problems. The road to Amman is also the first leg of the journey to Damascus (Syria) and Baghdad (Iraq). The surge in traffic has placed a heavy burden on demand for trucks; and the weight of traffic is far too heavy for the existing 220-mile (335-kilometer) Desert Highway. The road is too crowded and accidents are frequent. The tonnage it has to bear results in damage to the road surface itself. The future looks brighter with the building of a two-lane highway along the length of the route.

The Hejaz Railway, once limited to cargo traffic, has been extended to Aqaba to carry phosphate to the port. A line now also transports passengers between Damascus and Amman. There, the Jordan National Shipping Lines Company operates cargo ships between Aqaba and European ports as well as a car and passenger ferry to Nuweiba in the Sinai Peninsula.

Jordan now has radio and television broadcasting stations with a range covering the whole country and beyond. Both radio and television run Arabic and foreign-language channels (English on the radio; English, French and German on the television). Now, Radio Jordan transmits in English and Arabic.

The establishment of the Amirate of Transjordan in 1921 found the country with no daily newspapers at all. Today the Press is flourishing. There are several daily newspapers, including the *Jordan Times*, an English-language daily. There are also many weekly newspapers and magazines. The government maintains a national news agency to publish and distribute news about Jordan.

Telecommunications in Jordan have developed rapidly. Telephones (a rarity thirty years ago) are in use everywhere. The roadside emergency telephone network even uses solar-powered telephones, the first such system in the world. Jordan was one of

A steam locomotive on the Turkish-built Hejaz Railway.

the first Arab countries to link up with Arabsat the communications satellite launched by the Arab countries.

Better communications with the outside world have opened Jordan to increased tourist trade. Tourism is now an important element in the country's economy. The loss of the West Bank, with the much-visited holy sites in Jerusalem, Bethlehem and Nazareth hit Jordan's tourist trade hard but the government is concentrating on developing the attractions of the East Bank. These include many Old Testament sites as well as the splendors of Jerash and Petra. There is the Dead Sea, the wild beauty of Wadi Rum and the desert castles. The marine life and good winter climate of Aqaba attract many visitors. The Ministry of Tourism encourages the development of facilities for visitors and

One of the car and passenger ferries which operate between the Jordanian port of Aqaba and Nuweiba on the Sinai Peninsula.

runs its own rest-houses at many places of interest. These include the hot springs of Zarqa Main, above the Dead Sea, where there is a hotel and physiotherapy center.

Despite the tremendous growth in Jordan's economy since independence, the country is unable to survive solely on its own efforts. Arab oil-producing countries help with aid grants which have funded many development projects. United Nations money helps with the resettlement of the Palestinian refugees.

Jordanian workers abroad have also given an important boost to the economy. The money they send home (to help their families or to invest) amounts in total to vast sums. Most of these expatriate workers are employed in the rich Gulf states, which offer high salaries. Jordan's well-developed education system means that the country can supply the type of professional staff needed to run government offices, service industries and construction projects in the oil-producing states.

Jordan "imports" labor as well as "exporting" its own workers. Egyptian laborers form the backbone of the Jordanian building industry. Sri Lankan and Filipino workers fill many nursing and domestic jobs. Engineering and finance companies from all over the world are engaged in the rapid development of Jordan and these firms are increasingly co-operating with local businesses in joint projects.

13

Education and Health

Education has always been highly prized by the Arabs. Nowadays it is seen in Jordan as a vital step to a brighter and more secure future, both for the individual and the country. Parents make great sacrifices to ensure a good education for their children. They also make sure the children work hard at school and, at home, have every possible help with their studies.

Jordan is an exceptionally young country in more ways than one. The population is growing quickly, which means that about forty percent of the country's inhabitants are aged fifteen or less. The high percentage of children of school age, and successive waves of refugees, have placed great strain on the education system but now free education is available for every child.

Nursery schools are all privately-run. Compulsory free education begins with elementary school. Children can start school if they are aged at least five years eight months at the beginning of the school year. Pupils go to their first school for six years, moving to the secondary level at about twelve years old.

The school-leaving age is fifteen but most students continue their education after this age.

The school day starts and finishes early. A typical school day starts at 8:00 a.m. and finishes at 1:00 p.m., but where there is great pressure on the local school, children attend in two shifts. The first group study from 7:00 to 11:30 a.m.; and the second group from 1:00 to 5:30 p.m. Girls wear green or blue tunic dresses to go to school but boys do not have any special school uniform.

Arabic studies usually take up a large amount of the pupils time during their first years at school. The written language (classical Arabic) is complex. Not only is it very different from the spoken language, but each letter of the alphabet can be written in up to four different ways. The short vowel sounds are

A group of children in Amman. About forty percent of the population of Jordan is aged fifteen or less and for them education is free.

not usually written down, making reading difficult at first. Students also begin to learn their second language—English—at a young age. Later, they may go on to take a third language, usually French.

At the age of fifteen, students who want to continue their education have a choice. They can stay on at school and take the final school-leaving examination (the *Tawjihi*), which is also the university entrance examination. Or they can choose three years of technical education in the fields of industry, agriculture, commerce or nursing.

After the *Tawjihi,* students can apply to community colleges, where they will study practical subjects such as engineering, computer science, teacher training or social work. Courses usually last two years.

There are six universities in Jordan, but three are in the occupied West Bank and one (Mutah), near Kerak, is reserved for officers in the armed forces. Jordan University (in Amman) and Yarmouk University (in Irbid) are open to the ordinary student, but because places are very limited, students need to gain very high marks in their *Tawjihi* examinations to be sure of a place. As a result, most Jordanian students at university level (about seventy thousand of them) are studying abroad. Some win scholarships or grants but most pay their own fees.

One important result of widespread education and the opening of universities in Jordan has been a dramatic increase in the number of doctors practicing in the kingdom. This has brought about a great improvement in health care over the last few

The entrance to Jordan University, Amman.

decades and the building of hospitals or clinics in most centers of population.

Amman has modern hospitals and enough doctors to serve the needs of its population. The situation in the country as a whole is less good. Most doctors prefer to live and work in the capital, where they can run private practices. But the government has opened clinics and health centers throughout the country, and medical services are subsidized. Jordanians usually have to pay for health care but fees in government hospitals are kept fairly low. For the very poor, treatment is free.

Government workers have their own health insurance plan. Several sophisticated military medical centers provide health care for members of the armed forces and their families. Civilians needing special facilities are sometimes treated in these hospitals,

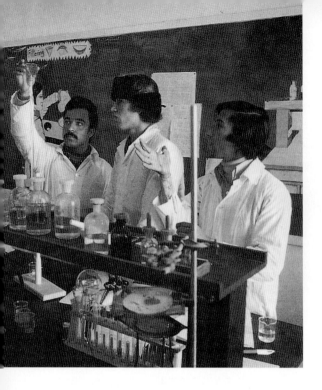

Research workers in a medical laboratory in Amman.

where heart transplants and micro-surgery have been carried out by teams of Jordanian surgeons.

While the number of doctors in Jordan is increasing all the time and many Jordanians study medicine in their own country or abroad, there is a severe shortage of trained nurses. Old prejudices still see nursing as a far from respectable profession and many families are reluctant to see their children become nurses. However, schools of nursing are gradually changing these ideas. Meanwhile, many of Jordan's nurses come from abroad.

Like most countries, Jordan has particular health problems. Its dusty atmosphere makes ear, nose and throat conditions common. Poor sanitation and ignorance of food hygiene can lead to dysentery, typhoid and cholera, but improved water supplies and health education are fighting these illnesses.

Similarly the many stray dogs prevent the effective control of rabies. As a result Jordanian children are brought up to fear and avoid dogs, which many Muslims also regard as unclean for religious reasons. In some parts of Jordan, mosquitoes spread malaria. Another common disease, bilharzia, is caught from the bilharzia snail, found in slow-moving water.

In the past, handicapped people in Jordan were usually cared for by their families. But now people are beginning to realize that this is not enough. The government and private charities are starting to look at ways of educating and training the disabled so that they can play a greater part in society. Services for the handicapped are still extremely limited but schools, day-care centers and rehabilitation centers are being developed, as well as improved medical services and preventive medicine.

14

Jordan's Wildlife

Jordan is a parched and barren-looking country for most of the year. But in the spring the bare brown hills turn unexpectedly green and, wherever rain has fallen, wild flowers grow in profusion. There are more than two thousand species of wild flower, including varieties found in northern Europe and the Mediterranean region, as well as in hotter countries. The fields of the hilly north are full of red anemones and every roadside blooms. Fruit-tree blossoms add to the colors of the landscape.

Although most of the country consists of apparently lifeless desert, there is also a great variety of wildlife in Jordan. Animals and birds associated with Europe, Asia and Africa survive in the kingdom, and the seas off the coast are an underwater paradise of tropical fish and coral.

However, many of the animals which used to live in Jordan are now extinct in the country, or no longer to be found in the particular places where they once lived in great numbers. Today, there are no lions, no cheetahs, no bears, no antelopes and no

Brightly-colored spring flowers near Jerash.

crocodiles. All these flourished in the region until the nineteenth century, when their natural habitats began to disappear. Grasslands were overgrazed by goats and camels, forests were chopped down and, worst of all, hunters began to use motor vehicles to track down their prey more effectively.

The Royal Society for the Conservation of Nature has been set up to protect Jordan's wildlife and to re-establish some of these animals. The RSCN now runs three reserves where animals are protected from hunters and encouraged to breed.

The first reserve was established at Shaumari, a fertile area in the desert near Azraq. Here, the Society has established a flourishing herd of Arabian oryx (long-horned antelopes which some people think are the original unicorns). The present herd started with the gift of two females and a male from the San Diego Zoo in the

United States, where the world's surviving oryx were living in captivity. Other desert animals which the RSCN is trying to re-establish in Jordan are the wild ass, several species of gazelle and the ostrich.

Azraq Oasis itself is the site of the Wetland Reserve, an area of pools, marshes, water meadows and dunes. The oasis is remarkable for its birdlife—over three hundred species of birds have been recorded there. At one time, during the migratory season, huge flocks stopped to drink at Azraq's pools. However, in recent years much of the water has been drained to supply Amman and other towns. As a result, the bird population has dwindled considerably. Water-birds especially can still be seen there, though, and these include fifteen species of duck; herons and egrets; cranes; ibises; flamingoes; pelicans; gulls; and many species of warbler.

Jordan's newest reserve is in the Wadi Mujib, a deep canyon running eastward from the Dead Sea. Gazelles, hyenas, wolves and porcupines live there and the Society wants to re-introduce the wild boar, which has become extinct in the area. Birds living in the Mujib include larks, wheatears, blackstarts, ravens, grackles and partridges.

Outside the reserves, Jordan's commoner animals include foxes, hares, badgers, hedgehogs and many smaller rodents. There are also wolves which occasionally come close to towns.

Among the many varieties of birds resident in the region are some colorful species, such as the Palestine sunbirds, hoopoes, rollers, bee-eaters and kingfishers.

Insects are not the nuisance in Jordan that they can be in more tropical climates, although malarial mosquitoes abound in the Jordan Valley. Scorpions inflict a poisonous and occasionally fatal sting, but they spend most of the day sheltering in the shade of stones. Some spiders in Jordan are huge but the only poisonous variety is the black widow, easily recognized by its shiny black body. Finger-length millipedes are common but harmless.

Even the desert teems with life. Big dung-beetles (the ancient Egyptian scarab) collect balls of dung and trundle them to burrows dug into the sand. Rats and gerbils survive in the desert. Many varieties of lizard also live there as elsewhere in Jordan. They range from tiny skinks to the desert monitor which can measure 53 inches (130 centimeters). Other reptiles include several harmless varieties of snake and two poisonous species—the horned viper and the Palestine viper.

Birds which live in the desert have adapted remarkably well to an inhospitable climate. Some desert birds breed only in those years when there is a certain amount of rain. They cover over their eggs with sand to shelter them from the sun. Another example of this adaptation is the sandgrouse. It carries water to its nestlings in its own belly feathers, which it soaks wherever it can find a pool.

Oases and even small pools teem with life, including migratory birds, animals which come to drink, red and blue dragonflies and other water-insects. Some tiny creatures only come to life after a downpour has created a small pool. When the water evaporates they bury themselves in the sand and lie dormant until the next rains.

The Dead Sea is lifeless but the waters of the Gulf of Aqaba are

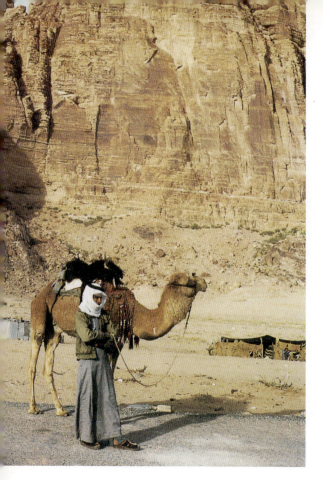

A Bedouin man with his camel. Much of Jordan is desert, or semi-desert, and camels are well able to survive in this environment.

rich in marine life. The sea here is warm all year round and, thanks to the efforts of the Aqaba port authority, clear enough for coral to grow. At one time, pollution was killing the coral and the fish which lived among it. But now good planning and protective measures have led to remarkably clean water even within the port itself.

Coral is the skeleton of a tiny animal; it grows outside the body, like a shell. These skeletons grow to form large coral reefs—a haven for brightly-colored tropical fish which live in and around these underwater cliffs.

Collecting live coral is banned because breaking pieces from the reef kills the animal. But at Aqaba it is easy to see the growing coral. Because the fringes of the reef reach into the shore, a snorkel is the only equipment needed to see the underwater panorama. Divers can explore the edge of the reef itself. There are also glass-bottomed boats which cruise slowly over the reef.

15

The Future

Jordan has repeatedly suffered from the conflicts and upheavals which have disturbed the Middle East since before the country's independence and which still beset the region. In particular, the West Bank remains under Israeli occupation and, despite repeated efforts, there is as yet no settlement to the Palestinian question.

There is no doubt that this small kingdom's future is closely linked with the future of the whole of the Middle East and that Jordan's very survival depends on its neighbors.

The Hashemite Kingdom is still a developing country. With few natural resources it is, for the moment, heavily reliant on support from other countries. This situation looks likely to continue for the foreseeable future. But the search continues for new mineral resources, such as oil, which would increase the national wealth and help the country to balance its budget.

Self-sufficiency for Jordan and a higher standard of living for its citizens may sometimes seem far in the future. But the government's development plans are doing much to improve the economy and the welfare of the people. Life for the ordinary Jordanian has changed radically in the years since independence. The people are now living in an increasingly modern state with all the economic and social benefits that brings.

GLOSSARY

Bedouin	Wandering Arabs who live in the deserts of the Middle East and move their homes according to the seasons.
dunum	Jordanian measure of land (one *dunum* equals 1,200 square yards).
hajj	Pilgrimage made to the holy city of Mecca by the followers of the Islamic religion.
jebels	The seven hills of Amman.
khamsin	Period of oppressive and dusty heat lasting for weeks at a time during the summer.
mosques	Muslim places of worship.
muhafazahs	Districts (governorates) that Jordan is divided into; there are eight *muhafazahs* in Jordan.
Muslims	Followers of the Islamic religion and of the teachings of Muhammad.
oasis	A fertile green area in the middle of the desert.
sheikh	Tribal leader.
siq	A narrow ravine passing through high cliffs of sandstone.
souk	Market.
wadi	A river that flows only after rain falls.

INDEX

A

Abbasid dynasty, 10
Abdullah Amir, 43
Abdullah, King, 11, 40
agal, 64
airport, 30, 80
Al Aqsa mosque, 33, 40, 75
alcohol, 53
Alexander the Great, 9, 32
Amman, 7, 17, 18, 21, 24-30, 31, 41, 63, 68, 71, 74, 78, 80, 81, 88, 89, 94
amphitheaters, 27, 36, 55, 75
Aqaba, 11, 16, 21, 23, 30, 45, 75, 78, 80, 82, 83
Aqaba, Gulf of, 13, 95-97
Arabs, Arabic, 10, 11, 15, 22, 33, 34, 40, 86, 87
Arab Legion, 11, 40, 44
Arab nationalists, 35, 39
Arab Revolt, 22, 35, 45
Arabsat, 83
archaeology, 21, 35-36, 37
armed forces, 41, 44, 89
arts, 55-56, 62
Awqaf, 45
Azraq, 22, 79, 93, 94

B

Babylonians, 9, 13, 32
Baghdad, 10
Baqaa, 30
Bedouin, 18, 37, 43, 46-47, 48-50, 62, 63, 68, 75, 96
Black September, 12
Britain, 11, 34, 35, 39, 42
British Mandate, 35, 39
building, 28, 29-30, 85
Burckhardt, Jean Louis, 36
Burgon, Dean, 37
Byzantines, 32, 33

C

calendar, 52
camels, 18, 43, 46-47, 93, 96
capital city (*see* Amman)
children, 59, 62, 70, 86
Christianity, 21, 27, 32, 54, 59, 60
Circassians, 10, 27, 50
clothes, 43, 64-65
communications, 80-83
courts, civil and religious, 45
cows, 67
crafts, 71-76
crops, 69-70
Crusaders, 21, 33

D

Damascus, 10, 16, 33, 75, 81, 82
Dead Sea, 7, 9, 17, 18, 19, 21, 78, 83, 95

101

Decapolis, 21, 36
desert, 13, 21, 22, 23, 46-47, 67, 92, 96
Desert Patrol, 43
drought, 55, 77
dubke (dance), 62

E
East Bank, 18, 21, 39, 46, 83
education, 20, 47, 85, 86-88
Egypt, 10, 12, 13, 33, 42
Eid al-Fitr, Eid al-Adha, 53
El Arish, 10

F
families, 57-62
farming, 18, 67-70, 77
Feisal, 11
fertilizers, 23, 78
flag, 39, 75
flowers, 20, 54-55, 92
food, 25, 60, 61-62
forests, 70, 93
France, 35

G
Galilee, Sea of (Lake Tiberias), 16-17
Gaza Strip, 40
Germany, 34
Gilead, 9, 21
Glubb, Sir John, 44
goats, 68-70, 93
government, 8, 42, 43-45, 66
Great Rift Valley, 16
Greater Syrian Desert, 22
Greeks, 13, 32
guerrillas, Palestinian, 18, 41

H
hajj (pilgrimage to Mecca), 54
Hasmoneans, 10
Hassan Crown Prince, 42
Hebron, 74
Hejaz Railway, 16, 70, 80, 82
Hijrah, 52
Hittin, Battle of, 33
hospitality, 48-50, 61
houses, 24, 30, 63
Hussein bin Talal, King, 11, 15, 21, 40, 42, 43, 48, 80

I
immams, 66
independence, 39, 99
industry, 8, 23, 77-80
Iraq, 7, 12, 13, 16, 21, 80, 81
Irbid, 7, 21, 88
irrigation, 17, 67
Islam, 15, 33, 52-54
Israel, 11, 12, 14, 21, 40, 41, 50, 98

J
Jebel Ammam, 30
Jebel Hussein, 30
Jebel Qal'a, 27
jebels, 24, 27
Jerash, 10, 21, 36, 55, 83
Jericho, 9
Jerusalem, 9, 10, 11, 14, 33, 40, 75, 83
jewelry, 26, 74-75
Jews, 39
Jordan Crafts Center, 76
Jordan Fertilizer Industry, 78
Jordan, Hashemite Kingdom of, 13, 39, 42, 77, 98

Jordan National Shipping Lines
    Company, 82
Jordan Petroleum Refinery, 78
Jordan River, 7, 10, 17, 19, 31, 39
Jordan Valley, 10, 16, 21, 41, 95

K
Karameh, 18
Kerak, 21, 33, 88
keyfiyah, 44, 64
khamsin, 55
King Hussein Bridge, 18
King Talal Dam, 80

L
Lake Nyasa, 16
Lake Tiberias (Sea of Galilee), 16, 17
languages, 15, 32
Lawrence, T.E., 11, 22
Lebanon, 12, 13, 33

M
Macedonians, 32
Madaba, 19, 71
Marka, 30
marriage, 58-59
Mecca, 10, 52
medicine, 79, 88-91
Medina, 52
Middle East, 31-32
Moses, 13, 38
mosques, 56, 60, 61, 63
mosquitoes, 91, 95
muhafazah, 43
Muhammad, Prophet, 33, 52
mukhtar (headman), 66
Muslims, 33, 34, 45, 50, 52, 59, 60, 68

N
Nabataeans, 9, 33, 36
Napoleon, 10
natural resources (minerals, potash,
    phosphate), 8, 78, 98
Noor, Queen, 42
nursing, 85, 90
Nuweiba, 82

O
oases, 23, 94, 95
October War, 12
oil, 77-78, 84-85, 98
Ottoman Turks, 10, 11, 33, 34

P
Palestine, 13, 14, 19, 33, 35, 39, 40, 51
Palestinians, 11, 12, 14, 28, 40, 50, 98
Palestine Liberation Organization, 12
parliament, 42, 43
Peake, Frederick (Pasha), 40, 44
Persian Gulf, 12
Persians, 13, 32
Petra, 10, 21, 33, 36, 37, 38, 48, 75, 83
Philadelphia, 27, 36
pigs, 68
pilgrims, 10, 34
pollution, 96
population, 7
property, 57, 58

R
Ramadan, 52
Red Sea, 13, 23, 74
refugee camps, 30, 51
refugees, 27, 50, 84, 85
religion, 8, 13, 15, 19, 21, 27

Religious Community Council, 45
roads, 17, 21, 30, 80
Romans, 10, 13, 21, 26, 32, 35-36

S
Saladin, 33
Salt, 20
Saudi Arabia, 7, 13, 16, 22, 55
Seleucids, 9, 10
Sharia (religious courts), 45
Shaumari, 93
sheep, 68, 70, 74
sheikh, 46
Sherif Hussein, 10, 11
Shobak, 33
shops, 24, 25, 60
Sinai Peninsula, 82
souks, 24, 26
sous, 25
streets, 28, 29
Sykes-Picot Agreement, 35
Syria, 7, 10, 12, 13, 16, 33, 75, 81

T
Talal, King, 11, 40, 42
Tawjihi, 88
tells, 36
temperature, 18, 19
tents, 18, 26
tourism, 23, 37, 71, 80, 83-84
Trajan, Emperor, 10
Transjordan, Amirate of (East Bank), 11, 35, 39, 40
tribes, 46-47
Turks, 10, 11, 13, 22, 33, 70

U
Umayyad dynasty, 10
United Nations (see also UNRWA), 40, 84
United States, 12
UNRWA (UN Relief and Works property Agency), 40, 51

V
villages, 18, 63-67

W
Wadi Araba, 21
Wadi Mujib, 21,94
Wadi Rum, 22, 75, 83
Wadi Shauib, 20
wadis, 20, 21
Wahdat, 30
War, First World, 22, 34, 35
War, Second Arab-Israeli, 14, 41
War, Second World, 39
water, 19, 23, 67
weather, 7, 18, 19, 54-56
West Bank, 9, 11, 12, 14, 15, 17, 31, 40, 41, 46, 74, 83, 88, 98
wildlife, 19, 23, 92-97

Y
Yarmouk, Battle of, 33
Yarmouk River, 7, 79, 80
Yarmouk University, 88

Z
Zarqa, 79
Zarqa River, 7, 21
Zarqa Main, 84